SHORT TALES
Fables

The Town Mouse
and the
Country Mouse

Adapted by Christopher E. Long
Illustrated by Mark Bloodworth

WAYLAND

First published in 2014 by Wayland

Copyright © 2014 Wayland

Wayland
338 Euston Road
London NW1 3BH

Wayland Australia
Level 17/207 Kent Street
Sydney, NSW 2000

Adapted Text by Christopher E. Long
Illustrations by Mark Bloodworth
Colours by Hi-Fi
Edited by Stephanie Hedlund and Rochelle Baltzer
Interior Layout by Kristen Fitzner Denton and Alyssa Peacock
Book Design and Packaging by Shannon Eric Denton
Cover Design by Alyssa Peacock

Copyright © 2008 by Abdo Consulting Group

A cataloguing record for this title is available at the British Library.
Dewey number: 398.2'452-dc23

Printed in China

ISBN: 978 0 7502 7835 5

Wayland is a division of Hachette Children's Books, an Hachette UK company.
www.hachette.co.uk

One day, Town Mouse went to visit his cousin.

Country Mouse welcomed Town Mouse into his home.

'Your home is small' Town Mouse said.

'But it's warm and peaceful' Country Mouse said.

8

Country Mouse served Town Mouse dinner.

'Everything is much better in town'
Town Mouse said.

'Come with me and I'll show you how to live' Town Mouse said.

'Your home is very large' Country Mouse said.

'Are you hungry, cousin?'
Town Mouse asked.

19

'Yes, I am' said Country Mouse.

'This is what we eat in town'
Town Mouse said.

Suddenly, the cousins heard barking.

25

They had to run and hide.

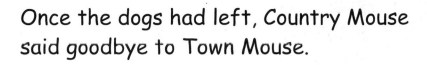

Once the dogs had left, Country Mouse said goodbye to Town Mouse.

'Better beans and bacon in peace than cakes in fear' he said.

The moral of the story is:

Better a little in safety, than much surrounded by danger.